Which Game Is the Best?

by Ms. Strong's class
with Tony Stead

capstone®
classroom

Soccer Is Best

by Alexa, Jasmine, Jayden, and Luke

I think soccer is the best game ever.

Soccer is a great game because
I can play it with my brother.

Soccer is also good because I can play it at my favorite park.

Soccer is a great game! Try it!

Baseball Is Best

by Briley, Damien, and Tobias

Which game do I like best?

That's easy! It's baseball.

I like baseball the best because you can run.

I also like baseball because I can hit the ball hard.

I think everyone should try this game! What game do you think is the best?